Harold is invited to
Donkey's fancy-dress party.

THE MYSTERY OF THE MISSING CAKE

CLAUDIA BOLDT

'Today is the perfect day for solving mysteries and eating cheese,' thinks Harold, tucked up warm in bed.

Though, for Harold every day was the perfect day for solving mysteries and eating cheese. He was certainly not your average fox.

Suddenly he hears a noise.
'Post for you,' calls Dad.

But he doesn't want to go.
'I won't know anybody who's going,' he says.

'You know Donkey. Besides, everyone loves
a party,' says Dad.

'I don't know. Well... at least I get
to make a costume.'

It's the day of the party and the forest is filling up with all sorts of monsters, rotten pumpkins and scary skeletons, but there is only one all-seeing eyeball.

At the party, all eyes are on the
ginormous birthday cake.
Everyone is eager to have a slice,
but Donkey wants to save the best for last.
'Paws off my cake,' shouts Donkey.

The birthday donkey
gets to choose all the party games.

The party is in full swing, when the pigs win the prize for the best dance routine.

10 8 9

Then it's time for Donkey's favourite game... Monster tag!

The lights go off. The game begins.

The lights go on. The cake is gone.

'Thief, criminal, robber, crook!' cries Donkey. 'Somebody stole MY CAKE!'

'Something isn't right!' says Harold and gets to work.

While the guests accuse each other of taking
the cake, Harold questions the suspects.
'This party just got a whole lot more interesting,'
thinks Harold. 'Someone must know something.'

Harold searches for clues,
but there are cake crumbs
all over the place.

'The evidence in the case of
the missing cake is inconclusive,'
announces Harold.

'Are all the witnesses telling
the truth?' he wonders.

One cake, nineteen guests,
one host and just as many witnesses.
Detective work isn't easy.

Donkey is very upset.
'I want to know who stole my cake.
As far as I can see it could have been anyone!'

'Not me,' says Harold. 'I only like cheese!'

'Everybody loves cake,' says Donkey.

'Not me.'

'Well, everybody but you loves cake,'
says Donkey. 'We'll never find out!'

'Everybody loves cake,' mumbles Harold.
'Everybody... loves... cake.'

'Yes, exactly. Everybody loves cake.
That's what I said,' cries Donkey.

'No, I mean yes! That's it. I know who did it!'

IT WAS

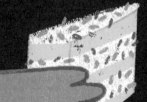

EVERYONE!

Harold solved the mystery!
Everyone had taken a tiny piece
of the cake until there was
none of it left.

SORRY!

NO, NO, NO.
I ONLY
HAD ONE
TINY PIECE.

I DIDN'T THINK
YOU'D NOTICE.

I WANT MORE.

ONE LITTLE
PIECE.

SORRY!

IT WAS ONLY
WAFER-THIN.

But Donkey is never sad for long!

'Who needs cake when all your friends are here to celebrate?' says Donkey. 'Hip, hip, hooray for Detective Harold.'

'Thank you, Donkey. This is one great party!' says Harold.

On the way home, Harold's Dad
wants to know all about the party.
'Did you have cake?' asks Dad.

'Nope.'

'A party without cake?
That's not a party!'

But Harold disagrees....

'It was the best party ever!'
And with that he falls asleep and
dreams of mysteries and cheese.